Analytical Argume

COURAGE

by Martina D. Hansson
illustrated by Alan Reingold

Table of Contents

INTRODUCTION

In life, people are often faced with difficult situations and decisions, and how they respond is a **testament** to their true nature and personality. It is common for people to consider **hypothetical** problems they might encounter and wonder how they would respond to them. Most people hope they would act bravely in a crisis or do the right thing if caught in an **ethical dilemma**, but it's impossible for them to know for sure until they are placed in those situations.

For most people, a decisive moment is a moment of truth. When forced to make a decision in light of a tragedy or conflict, people reveal a lot about themselves. Some people will risk their lives to help others; some will take a position they don't believe in solely to be liked by others; some will run away and refuse to get involved; and others will remain uninvolved but take advantage of those who are affected by the situation.

ethical dilemma a problem related to doing what is right

The same is true for characters in literature. As the plot unfolds in a work of fiction, characters will face challenges and decisions, and how they respond and change in reaction to these situations reveals their true nature to readers. For readers to gain a better understanding of the characters, they must consider the characters' thoughts, feelings, and true motivations in relation to what they say and do.

But just as in life, not everyone will share the same opinion about a person's behavior. No matter what a person does, other people will perceive his or her actions differently depending on their own views. What one person may dismiss as a cowardly response, another person may praise as a smart reaction.

The following stories all include characters who respond to difficult situations in their lives. Carefully consider the details of each story to determine what the characters' actions reveal about them.

SOFIA

PATRICIA

STEPHEN

INTO THE FIRE

Sofia hurried along in the predawn light of Lowell, Massachusetts, on her way to the textile mill. Like most days, her shift started at five o'clock, and she could not be tardy. Mr. Mitchell, the owner of the mill, often told his "girls" they could be replaced "in less time than it takes to sew a button on a dress." Just as Sofia approached Mrs. Winchester's boardinghouse, a new worker, a girl named Madeline, dashed out the door and almost collided with her.

"Oh, I'm so sorry. I'm in a rush this morning and I didn't see you coming," the girl quickly apologized.

"Don't worry, Madeline. I'm rushing along myself. Shall we walk to the mill together?" Sofia asked.

Secretly, Madeline was thrilled by this offer, but she **squelched** her enthusiasm for fear of looking like a giddy little girl. It was rare for an older, more experienced worker, especially a seventeen-year-old like Sofia, to pay any attention to a newly hired, younger worker, and Madeline didn't want to make a bad impression.

So, she calmly held her **composure** and replied, "Certainly."

They walked briskly and silently through the damp coolness of late-April New England until Sofia, noting the girl's nervousness, asked, "How are things going? My first few weeks were horrendous. Once, I almost ruined a bolt of fabric because I stitched the wrong side. My supervisor caught it and helped me redo it. But I had to give up a day off."

"I haven't made any mistakes quite like that," Madeline said, suppressing a snicker. "I'm getting faster, too. But the work sure is tiring."

"At least tomorrow is Sunday," said Sofia. "I'm going to write a letter to my Pa. Why don't you come to my boardinghouse and we can write letters together?"

"Um . . . certainly!" said Madeline, no longer worrying about keeping her composure.

Before long, the girls joined the crowd of other workers, nearly all of them girls and young women in their teens and early twenties, trudging through the only door of the **formidable** brick building. Rows of intricate looms stretched the length of the dimly lit room, and a wooden bin of discarded scraps occupied one corner. Sofia's loom was in the row against the wall, about halfway down the row, and Madeline's was a few spaces away from hers.

The girls smiled wanly at each other as they parted company, girding themselves for the long day ahead. They took their positions at their looms, and then under the watchful eye of their supervisor, Mrs. McLaughlin, they began their fourteen-hour workday. *At least tomorrow is Sunday*, thought Madeline.

The girls worked without talking, but their silence was filled by the rhythmic beat of clicking **shuttles** and pumping foot **treadles**.

Several hours into the workday, Sofia slouched over from exhaustion. The air suddenly felt heavy in her lungs and made it hard for her to breathe. She inhaled deeply, hoping to take in a wave of oxygen, but instead she absorbed a cloud full of smoke. Turning, she looked toward the scrap bin in the corner and saw that it was consumed by flames. Bright red tentacles darted and leaped up from the bin and toward the wall.

"Fire, fire! The scrap bin is on fire!" she screamed.

Pandemonium instantly erupted as three-dozen girls shoved past each other and raced to escape. With all eyes aimed toward the lone door, they pushed through the rows of looms, knocking over equipment and sending it crashing to the floor.

shuttles holders designed to carry thread across a loom
treadles parts of a weaving loom operated by the foot to produce a circular motion

Sofia made her way through the mob of shrieking girls and was just two feet from the door when she heard Madeline's panicked wail rise up from deep inside the room.

"My foot—it's stuck in the treadle! I can't get it loose!"

Sofia squirmed and craned her neck behind her as the throng of stampeding textile workers shoved her forward. She turned to look for Madeline and watched as the other girls rushed past her, deaf to Madeline's pleas.

"My foot—it's stuck!"

It was as if Madeline's cries were in a frequency only Sofia could hear. Without a moment's pause for her own well-being, Sofia swiftly headed back in the direction of the fire, pushing through the escaping workers as if swimming upstream against a rushing current, to find the trapped girl.

Madeline was frantically wiggling and twisting her leg, but her foot remained stuck in the machine. When she saw Sofia approaching, she waved her away.

"Go, get out—save yourself! There isn't any time to waste! Death may be my fate today, but it doesn't have to be yours!" Madeline cried.

"And it won't be yours, either," Sofia replied sternly.

Sofia quickly crouched down under the loom and saw Madeline's ankle wedged between two thick wooden treadles.

"On my count of three, you pull while I push the treadle. One, two, three!" Sofia cried loudly.

"AH!" cried Madeline, louder still.

Sofia tried again to separate the pieces of wood with her hands, but they were too heavy.

Squinting against the heavy smoke above her, Sofia's eyes roamed the rapidly burning factory walls for something, anything, to use as a lever. "Your shuttle, of course!"

Right away, Sofia wedged the shuttle between the wooden pieces of the treadle to pry them apart.

"One, two, three!" cried Sofia again, using all her remaining strength to push down on the lever. A satisfying crack echoed around her as the treadles broke and fell to the side. Madeline was free from her **shackle**.

Sofia grabbed Madeline's arm and pulled the frightened girl up from the ground. "Come with me—we have to hurry."

Sofia wrapped her arm around Madeline's waist and supported her as she limped toward the door. They heard Mrs. McLaughlin calling their names from outside the doorway and stumbled together through the **threshold** toward her voice.

Once outside, Mrs. McLaughlin shoved them away from the fire-engulfed building just in time for a chunk of cornice to come crashing down into the space where they had just stood. She sat the dazed girls down on the ground and carefully inspected them, wiping soot from their faces and hands.

The girls coughed fitfully.

"You girls are lucky to be alive, and lucky to have not been burnt," said Mrs. McLaughlin. "You certainly inhaled a lot of smoke, but that's nothing you can't recover from. And your ankle, too, will be just fine after it has time to heal, Madeline."

Madeline looked admiringly at Sofia. "I only made it out because of Sofia. If she hadn't turned around when I called out, I would still be in there. I owe my life to her."

Sofia shook her head and humbly dismissed the praise. "Please don't feel **indebted** to me," she said. "All I did was help a friend."

TOGETHER AND EQUAL

Papa, Mama, you may disapprove of what I have to say, but I need to speak my piece."

Henry and Janet Henderson looked up from their dinner as Patricia, their thirteen-year-old, and youngest of four, continued.

"The other night when I went to Naomi's house, Mr. and Mrs. Washington had a meeting of the local **NAACP** chapter. Mr. Dawkins from the NAACP headquarters said they want some volunteers to be the first black students to integrate the junior high school. Naomi already agreed, and I want to do it, too." She set her jaw and looked hopefully at her father.

Mr. Henderson placed his hands flat on the table and looked directly at Patricia. He seemed calm, but Patricia recognized the fire in his eyes.

"Absolutely not. Don't get me wrong—I'm 100 percent for **integration**, but too many other people don't agree with us yet. I won't have you putting yourself in that kind of trouble."

"But Papa, I'll be with Naomi and seven other students. You have to understand that this is important to us. We want things to be different for the people in this town."

Always the calm in the center of the storm, Mrs. Henderson looked lovingly from her daughter to her husband.

"Please listen to your daughter, Henry. It's 1959, and you know it's high time for school integration in Virginia. The whole idea of **separate but equal** is nothing but bunk. Patricia's school has worn, outdated books, and some of the kids have to sit on the floor because the classrooms are so crowded. Never mind the paint on the walls that's as old as the hills. And she's forced to ride the bus clear across town every day to go to the black school when she could walk right down the street to the white school instead."

NAACP National Association for the Advancement of Colored People
integration a policy whereby black students attend the same school as white students
separate but equal a term used to describe school segregation; supporters claimed that even though black students attended schools separate from white students, they received equal treatment, but that usually was not the case

"I'm not denying that the white school is better stocked and better staffed, but what about your safety, Patricia?" asked Mr. Henderson. "You can talk all you want about your principles of integration, but I have principles as your father. The main one is to keep you safe. There may be picket lines and riots, and I don't want you in the middle of that kind of scene. I don't want you getting hurt, or worse. Think about what would happen to your mother and me if something happened to you."

Patricia knew that look in her father's eyes, too. "Papa, I know I'm still your little girl, but I'm not so little anymore. I can handle myself. Besides, we're getting training to deal with those kinds of situations. I understand what might happen, but it's a risk I am prepared to take. We will have federal marshals to escort us, along with NAACP organizers and members of the community. I hope that you two will join the group, too."

Patricia and her mother both looked at Papa as he grumbled to himself, picking up a forkful of mashed potatoes while he considered the information. Awaiting his verdict was torture, but Patricia willed herself to stay still and quiet. Finally, one of his grumbles turned into **intelligible** English.

"Oh, all right—you do what you have to do. I still don't support this decision, but I'm not going to stop you, either. You just better be careful and keep yourself safe."

Immediately, Patricia sprung up from her seat and hugged both of her parents. "Oh, thank you, thank you! I'm going to tell Naomi right now!"

After two intense weeks of training and planning, the time finally came for the integration walk-in. The **procession** started in front of Naomi's house to calls of encouragement from neighbors. But as the group proceeded toward the school, the onlookers they passed began to hurl more and more insults.

"Stay with your own kind!" yelled one onlooker.

"Race-mixing is communism!" called another.

The protesters carried signs that said similar things, and others that were far worse.

Patricia and her friends maneuvered through the crowd, which seemed to grow larger as they progressed along the road to the school. The group walked as quickly as they could but with dignity.

13

"Do not show fear," Patricia reminded Naomi. "And stay calm no matter what. Remember that they are looking for any reason to keep us from going in."

At the school, the marshals moved in closer; Patricia noticed a wall of grim-faced National Guard soldiers on either side of the sidewalk leading up to the front steps. Over her shoulder, she saw a small contingent of supporters applauding as the girls climbed the steps. "We shall overcome!" they sang.

Then *plunk, plunk, plunk*! Two young men broke through the mass of angry protesters and began chucking eggs at the first black students to enter the junior high school.

Without even flinching, the girls dodged the small white missiles and kept right on walking. Then, Patricia and Naomi squeezed each other's hands even tighter, gave each other a determined look, and pushed through the door into the school.

The following Saturday, the NAACP group met again at the Washingtons' home, and this time, Mr. and Mrs. Henderson joined the group. Mr. Dawkins asked all of the students for reports on their week.

Patricia listened to the other students tell about the **taunts** and jeers and the pranks pulled against them. When a girl told about her fear of being physically injured, Patricia noticed that her father gave her one of his looks, but it wasn't the one she had expected. It was one of respect.

When it was Patricia's turn, she talked about her pride being sore from the wounds inflicted upon it. She talked about her anger at being treated poorly. She talked about her indignation about the injustice. But she also talked about one white girl who had reminded her of the purpose behind their cause.

"She passed me a note on my first day of school that said, simply, 'Be brave. I believe in you.' It was a small act, but it restored my hope that things will change, soon, for us and for others. We will achieve together and equal as long as we believe we can."

Everyone in the room nodded their heads in agreement and heartily applauded Patricia's words.

BREAKING THE SILENCE

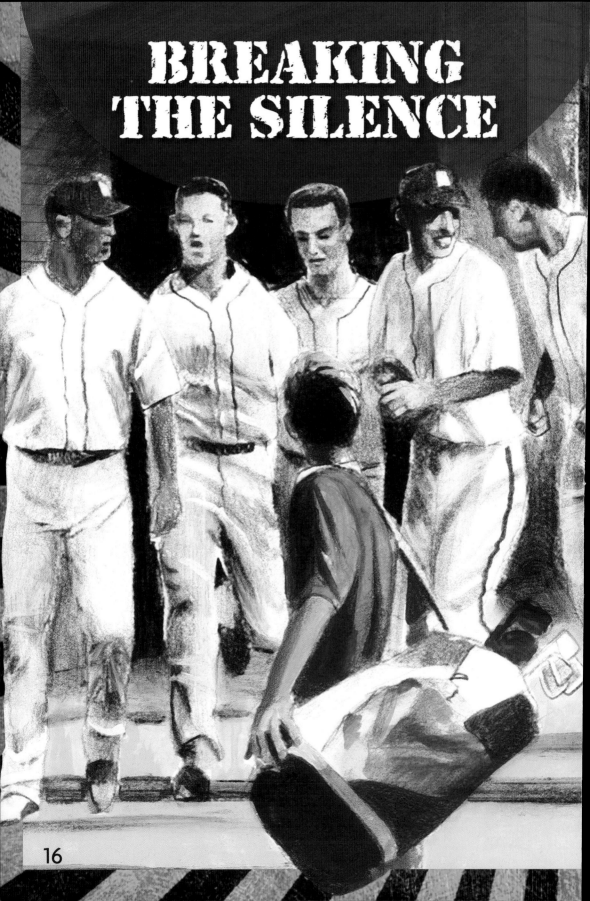

Ten minutes after the final bell, the hallways of Kennedy High School were eerily quiet and empty. Stephen was always amazed at how quickly the chaotic mob of students abandoned the building; it was as if a herd of wild horses was racing across the Russian Steppes. The only kids left were ones like him who stayed around for a sport or a club meeting. And with only two more days before the baseball team's regional championship, Stephen wouldn't get to leave for another four hours.

Turning the corner of the hallway outside the gym, Stephen saw a few of his teammates and joined them on their way to the locker room.

"What's up, Stephano?" asked Jared, the team's star pitcher. "Ready to put those clowns from Bayview into their place on Thursday?" Stephen hated it when Jared called him Stephano, but he had assigned pet nicknames to all the starters, and it seemed to bring the team good luck. So, Stephen put up with being Stephano once in a while. The boys changed into their practice gear and then headed for the field.

In front of the door stood a tall, lanky kid wearing a blue polo shirt and pleated khaki pants. He saw the baseball team heading toward him and quickly moved to the side, but not quick enough.

"Watch where you're going!" roared Jared, as some of the other kids on the team snickered.

"I'm sorry," said Zachary, more out of habit than for any other reason. "I was just waiting for my friend."

Stephen knew this would be trouble. For some reason, a couple of the baseball players and a few other kids in the school took pleasure in picking on Zachary. He was incredibly smart and apparently a golf whiz, but he had a hard time making friends because of his **quirky** habits and rules.

Everything to Zachary had a reason and a purpose. If he was wearing blue, it wasn't because it was the first shirt he pulled from the closet or because that's what he felt like wearing; it was because it was Tuesday and he always wore blue on Tuesdays.

Stephen never understood what the big deal was because in some ways, he wished he could be so organized. Maybe then his parents wouldn't nag him so much. And besides, he knew that Zachary never did anything to bother other people. They weren't looking for a fair fight; they just wanted to prove their domination.

Stephen watched as Jared stepped in front of Zachary and moved in close to his face.

"What's that, Mr. **Bogey**; you have friends? I thought your only friends were Mr. Five-Iron, Mr. Putter, and all your little clubs here," he said, kicking Zachary's golf bag. "Speaking of which, maybe I should introduce your little friends to my *big* friends."

Jared grabbed the bag, took out each club one by one, and handed it to a teammate.

When he pulled the last club from the bag and tried to pass it to Stephen, Stephen hesitated.

"Come on, Jared," Stephen said. "We don't have time for this. Coach is going to be mad if we're not on the field by three-thirty. Let's just go."

"Oh, don't be such a baby, Stephano. Just take the stupid club."

Stephen reluctantly took the club and stood there with it at his side.

"What's your policy on broken clubs?" Jared asked Zachary as he held the club above his knee.

"Don't do this, Jared—just leave him alone," chimed in Stephen, stepping between Zachary and Jared.

"Please don't break that club," Zachary pleaded. "I won't be able to play if something happens to it."

18   bogey a golf term meaning a score of one shot over par for the hole

"I guess you'll just have to learn to play a *real* sport, then," Jared said, as he bent the club and threw it on the ground in front of Zachary.

Devin and Jamal bent the clubs in their hands. Those three walked from the locker room **braying** like donkeys as Zachary sank to his knees on top of his ruined clubs.

The rest of the team kept their clubs whole but still threw them down at Zachary before heading out to practice.

Stephen knelt down next to Zachary. "I'm so sorry," he said. "They shouldn't have done this to you. We'll get you new clubs."

"I'm used to those guys being mean," Zachary replied. "But this is different. I can only play with these clubs. And they know that I won't turn them in because then they'll *really* do something horrible to me."

Stephen understood Zachary's dilemma and felt that he, too, was in an impossible position. It would be easy for him to stay quiet and ensure that his friends and teammates avoided punishment. They were some of the best players on the team and losing them before regionals would be devastating. Yet, he also knew that being a silent witness to the events that had just transpired would make him almost as guilty as the actual **perpetrators**.

"I'll figure something out," he told Zachary, running out to the field before his teammates got suspicious about his absence.

During practice, Stephen dropped an easy pop fly and barely hit the ball out of the infield. No matter how hard he tried, he couldn't pry his thoughts of Zachary from their grip on his brain. A burning hole in the pit of his stomach grew inside of him until it felt like a flesh-eating virus was **devouring** him from the inside out. As much as he dreaded the consequences, Stephen knew what he had to do.

The next day, during his first period class, Stephen asked to be excused. But instead of walking toward the restroom, he made his way to the main office. Shortly after he explained to the secretary why he was there, the principal called him into his office.

"I hear you have something to tell me, Stephen," the principal said, with both concern and compassion in his voice.

"Yes, sir. It's about a few of my baseball teammates. You see, yesterday . . ."

Stephen told his story, and just as he feared, Jared, Devin, and Jamal were suspended and forced to sit out the playoff game, which Kennedy lost. Stephen took a lot of heat from his teammates for being a "traitor," though Coach stood behind him.

In addition, the three troublemakers needed to replace Zachary's damaged clubs. Thereafter, Jared no longer called Stephen "Stephano," and he wouldn't even look him in the eye.

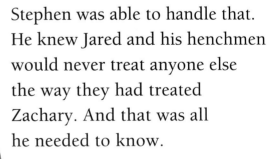

Stephen was able to handle that. He knew Jared and his henchmen would never treat anyone else the way they had treated Zachary. And that was all he needed to know.

Read and Evaluate Arguments About Characters' Actions

Now that you have read the three fictional stories, read three writers' arguments about how the characters in the story responded to difficult situations and decisions. Each writer was given the same writing prompt, highlighted below. The writers have different claims, yet each one provides a good example of how to write a strong argument. A well-written argument is backed up by reasons, uses transition words to connect ideas and paragraphs, and has a concluding statement. In the first essay, annotations have been added to help you identify these important parts of an argument.

Argument Writing Prompt

Think about how Sofia, Patricia, and Stephen act and respond to the events in each story. Choose an event from each story in which the main character makes a decision to act. How would you describe the characters' actions in light of their circumstances? State your claim and defend it using evidence from the text.

Characters with Courage

In each of the three stories, "Into the Fire," "Together and Equal," and "Breaking the Silence," the main character responds with courage to a difficult situation. Sofia puts her own life in danger to save another person. Patricia risks her own safety for a cause she believes in. And Stephen makes a huge sacrifice to protect someone else. All three are brave to make the decisions they do.

First, in "Into the Fire," Sofia risks her own life by going back to save Madeline. Sofia could have made the selfish decision to exit to safety. She might have assumed one of the other girls would help Madeline or that a firefighter would rescue her. Instead, with her safety only steps away, Sofia goes back toward the fire to find her friend. It is a difficult fight just to get there, but she is brave and selfless. As the story says, "Without a moment's pause for her own well-being, Sofia swiftly headed back in the direction of the fire." To do this, she has to push through a mob of escaping workers, "as if swimming upstream against a rushing current."

It <u>also</u> takes courage for Sofia to stay and help Madeline once she sees that her friend is stuck in the machine. Sofia doesn't give up when she can't move the treadle. She quickly finds a tool to pry it open. Even though she can hardly see through the thick smoke, she perseveres. Thanks to Sofia's determination, both girls make it out of the building alive.

> The writer uses linking words to connect reasons and ideas.

<u>Similarly</u>, in "Together and Equal," Patricia shows courage in a dangerous situation. She chooses to participate in the integration walk-in despite possible harm to herself. Dealing with "picket lines and riots," she says, "is a risk [she is] prepared to take." Patricia is committed to the belief that all students should receive the same treatment. So, she is willing to fight for the rights of black students to attend the white school. It is time for her community to change, and she wants to be part of that change.

> The writer uses evidence from the text to support a reason.

It is <u>also</u> courageous of Patricia to go forward with her decision even though her father disapproves. Mr. Henderson is worried about his daughter's safety. He doesn't want Patricia to participate in the walk-in.

The writer continues to use linking words to connect reasons and ideas.

Patricia could have given in to her father's concern for his "little girl," but instead she shows him how passionate she is about her cause. <u>Plus</u>, she shows how brave she is when she and her friends walk into the white school. She keeps her dignity even when an angry mob shouts insults and throws eggs at Patricia's group. Patricia keeps cool in an explosive situation. This in itself is an act of courage.

<u>Like</u> Patricia, Stephen, the main character in "Breaking the Silence," stands up for what he thinks is right. When Stephen witnesses some other players on the baseball team bully Zachary, he has to decide if he should report them or keep quiet. He knows that what they did was wrong, but there is a lot at stake if he reports them. For one thing, Stephen is likely to become very unpopular with his teammates. He also risks hurting the team's chances in the playoffs. Stephen faces his dilemma with resolve: "As much as he dreaded the consequences, Stephen knew what he had to do." So, Stephen's decision to tell the principal about what happened

is an act of courage. Instead of doing what's best for him, he does the right thing for Zachary. By doing so, he loses not only an important game but also the approval of his peers.

All three characters are brave in different ways, yet all are willing to make sacrifices. Sofia's bravery fits the heroic model; she puts herself in harm's way to save someone's life. Patricia also risks potential physical harm by standing up for and defending an important principle, so that others will reap the benefits. Finally, Stephen shows his courage by defending another person, even though it comes at a cost to him.

The writer provides a concluding statement or section.

ARGUMENT 2

Foolish Decisions

Each of the main characters in "Into the Fire," "Together and Equal," and "Breaking the Silence" is faced with a difficult choice. Though their actions seem courageous, they risk hurting themselves and others. In each case, the characters could have gotten the same positive results with less risk.

In "Into the Fire," Sofia is brave to go back to save Madeline, but she risks both their lives in the process. Rather than find a firefighter who would know what to do, Sofia fights her way back to Madeline through a mob of "shrieking girls." It also takes a while for Sofia to free Madeline's foot from the treadle, as her "eyes roamed the rapidly burning factory walls for something, anything, to use as a lever." In the meantime, valuable time is lost. Both girls could have died. Sofia makes a snap decision in a moment of crisis without considering the consequences.

Unlike Sofia, Patricia has time to think about the risks of her decision in "Together and Equal." She joins a local chapter of the NAACP and volunteers to participate in an integration walk-in. Her father warns her about the dangers of "picket lines and riots." He does not want her "getting hurt, or worse." Yet, Patricia doesn't seem to care about her own safety or her parents' concerns. During the walk-in, protesters throw eggs at Patricia and the other students. They are also jeered at and taunted. Though Patricia shows courage by joining the walk-in, she does not consider less dangerous ways of protesting. Instead, she puts herself in a situation where there is a risk of physical harm.

Stephen's situation is different. He does not face the same type of risk as Sofia and Patricia do; however, he does suffer the consequences of his bravery. Even though Stephen feels sorry for Zachary, he doesn't try very hard to stop his teammates when they bully Zachary. He even stands by when they break Zachary's golf clubs. It is no surprise that Stephen begins to have feelings of guilt after the incident. He feels as if "a flesh-eating virus was devouring him from the inside out." So, the very next day he reports the incident to the principal. As a result, his teammates are suspended and his high school baseball team loses the regional championship.

Though Stephen does the right thing, he doesn't think his decision through. If he had waited just one more day to report his teammates, he could have done the right thing for Zachary, his team, and the students of Kennedy High.

Important decisions must be made with a lot of thought, even in a crisis situation. Sofia, Patricia, and Stephen acted rashly and did not think through the consequences of their actions. They could have had the same positive results without endangering themselves and others or letting other people down.

Worth the Risk

In the stories "Into the Fire," "Together and Equal," and "Breaking the Silence," Sofia, Patricia, and Stephen all make decisions that place them in dangerous situations. But their choices are ultimately worth the risk. Sofia risks her own life to save someone else's, Patricia puts her safety at risk to support a cause she believes in, and Stephen stands up against his peers to protect another person.

To start with, Sofia's choice to go back toward the fire to save Madeline wasn't very smart. But, if she hadn't gone back in, Madeline might not have made it out alive. It is very possible that no one else would have helped Madeline. It is also possible that since part of the building had collapsed, the firefighters would not have been able to get back in to save her.

Patricia also puts herself in a dangerous situation by being part of an integration walk-in at a school for white students only. She ignores her father's concerns and joins the other black students marching into the school. She does this knowing that she could get seriously hurt by angry protesters. This certainly isn't the safest choice for a girl in middle school to make.

However, Patricia's decision to stand by her cause is ultimately worth the risks she takes. Patricia's courageous actions end up paving the way for black students to receive better schooling. Not only do the girls successfully make their way into the school, but they also generate a sense of change that will likely spread to other schools and communities.

Just as Patricia wants equal treatment for the black students, Stephen thinks his classmate Zachary deserves better treatment from his peers. Stephen objects to the way his teammates on the baseball team taunt Zachary and break his golf clubs. He makes a decision to put an end to their bullying by reporting their actions to the principal. By doing this a day before a championship game, Stephen takes a big risk. He knows that his teammates will probably be suspended. He also knows this means his team will lose the game.

Still, it is worth it for Stephen to risk the approval of his teammates and lose the championship in order to do what he feels is right. If he had kept his silence, it would have sent a message to his teammates that what they did to Zachary was acceptable. And, most likely, they would have continued to bully Zachary, and many other students, even more.

Many people do brave things that may also be perceived as foolish, but as all three of these characters show, their bold actions often lead to worthwhile results. The characters in these stories share a concern for others and a belief in doing what's right.

EVALUATE THE ARGUMENT TEXTS

Reread each argument piece and evaluate it using the rubric below as a guide. Write your evaluation of each essay on a separate piece of paper. Did the writers include the important elements?

Argument Writing Rubric

Argument Traits	4	3	2	1
The writer states a strong opinion, position, or point of view.				
The writer supplies well-organized reasons that support his or her opinion using facts, concrete examples, and supporting evidence from the text.				
The writer links opinions and reasons using words, phrases, and clauses.				
The writer provides a concluding statement or section that supports the position.				

4—exemplary; 3—accomplished; 2—developing; 1—beginning

GLOSSARY

braying   (BRAY-ing) *verb* laughing loudly in a disrespectful way (page 19)

composure   (kum-POH-zher) *noun* self-control (page 5)

devouring   (dih-VOW-uh-ring) *verb* eating with great hunger (page 20)

formidable   (FOR-mih-duh-bul) *adjective* great in size (page 6)

hypothetical   (hy-puh-THEH-tih-kul) *adjective* possible or potential, as pertains to an idea (page 2)

indebted   (in-DEH-ted) *adjective* owing someone for something the person did (page 9)

intelligible   (in-TEH-lih-jih-bul) *adjective* able to be understood; clear (page 12)

pandemonium   (pan-duh-MOH-nee-um) *noun* disorder and uproar (page 6)

perpetrators   (PER-peh-tray-terz) *noun* people who do something wrong (page 19)

procession   (pruh-SEH-shun) *noun* a group of people moving forward in an orderly way, as in a parade (page 13)

quirky   (KWER-kee) *adjective* related to odd mannerisms (page 17)

shackle   (SHA-kul) *noun* something that prevents one's freedom, such as a cuff placed on the wrist or ankle of a prisoner (page 8)

squelched   (SKWELCHT) *verb* suppressed; held inside (page 5)

taunts   (TAUNTS) *noun* insults (page 14)

testament   (TES-tuh-ment) *noun* proof or evidence that something is true (page 2)

threshold   (THRESH-hold) *noun* entranceway, such as a doorway (page 8)

ANALYZE THE TEXT

Questions for Close Reading

Use facts and details from the text to support your answers to the following questions.

- What can you infer about Sofia and Madeline's relationship prior to the fire? Cite specific details from the text to support your response.

- What is the significance of the note a girl gives to Patricia during her first week at the integrated school? How does this relate to the overall theme of the story?

- Reread the last two paragraphs of Argument 1. Why does the writer claim that Stephen's decision was courageous in light of his circumstances?

- Reread Argument 2 and explain the writer's central claim. How does the writer support this claim with reasons and evidence from the stories?

Comprehension: Sequence of Events

The plot of a short story unfolds in a sequence, or chronological order, of events. Choose one of the short stories. Fill in the sequence chart to identify the most important event from the beginning, middle, and end of the story.

Beginning

Middle

End